PINOCCHIO

by Pinocchio

To Ann-Janine

From us both
and from Pinocchio
with our love and thanks

First published in hardback in Great Britain byHarperCollins Children's Books in 2013
HarperCollins Children's Books is a division of HarperCollins Publishers Ltd,
77-85 Fulham Palace Road, Hammersmith, London, W6 8JB.

The HarperCollins website address is: www.harpercollins.co.uk

1

Text copyright © Michael and Clare Morpurgo 2013
Illustrations copyright © Emma Chichester Clark 2013

ISBN 978-0-00-758849-7

Michael Morpurgo and Emma Chichester Clark assert the moral right
to be identified as the author and illustrator of this work.

Printed and bound in China

MICHAEL MORPURGO
PINOCCHIO
by Pinocchio

Illustrated by Emma Chichester Clark

HarperCollins *Children's Books*

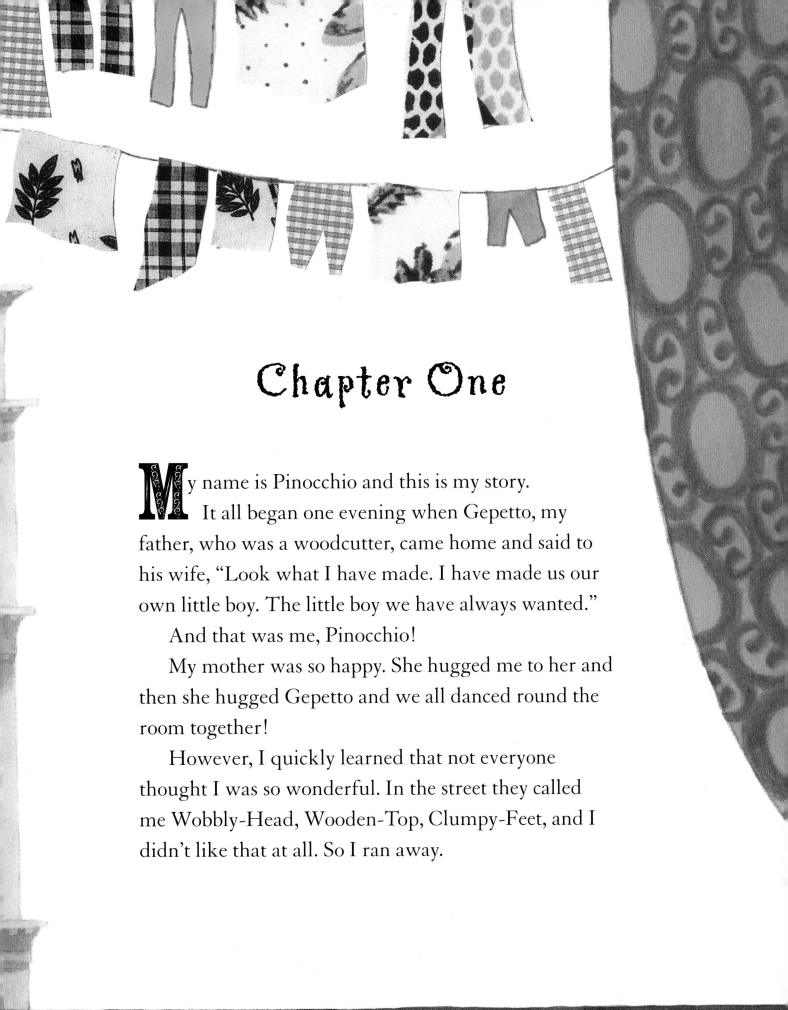

Chapter One

My name is Pinocchio and this is my story.

It all began one evening when Gepetto, my father, who was a woodcutter, came home and said to his wife, "Look what I have made. I have made us our own little boy. The little boy we have always wanted."

And that was me, Pinocchio!

My mother was so happy. She hugged me to her and then she hugged Gepetto and we all danced round the room together!

However, I quickly learned that not everyone thought I was so wonderful. In the street they called me Wobbly-Head, Wooden-Top, Clumpy-Feet, and I didn't like that at all. So I ran away.

How I could run! I ran in leaps and bounds, tickety tackety,
down the cobbled street, dodging this way and that until Signor
Biffo the big policeman caught me and took me home to Mama
and Papa.

"Please never run away again, Pinocchio," said Mama,
hugging me to her.

"Tomorrow you will go to school," said Papa. "You will like it there
and you will make lots of friends."

But I didn't like it there at all and I didn't make lots of friends,
so, although I loved Mama and Papa, I decided to run away again
and see the world and make my fortune.

Chapter Two

Once again I ran in leaps and bounds, tickety tackety, down the cobbled street and out into the countryside.

Soon it started to rain and I began to feel cold and hungry. So when I saw a little cottage with the door standing open, I went in. Imagine how pleased I was to find some bread on the table and a warm fire crackling in the hearth. Lickety split, I ate the bread and curled up by the fire to warm myself.

Then I heard a little voice. "Cri-cri," it went, and I saw a tiny cricket crawling up the wall beside me. To my surprise he said, "Running away, little boy, is always a foolish idea – it never makes you happy and it makes your Mama and Papa very sad."

"What do you know?" I cried. "I want to be free, to see the world, to do what I like."

"Go ahead then, Pinocchio, but you will turn into a donkey and people will laugh at you even more. You'll get into all sorts of trouble and you might even end up in prison."

"I don't need any lessons from you, a stupid talking cricket," I shouted. "Stop it right now!"

But he wouldn't.

I know it was wrong, but at that moment I didn't care – I picked up a log and threw it at him. It hit him much harder than I meant it to.

"Cri-cri," he cried, and disappeared.

Then I felt very bad. I lay down by the fire and sobbed. I fell asleep and when I woke up I found my feet had been burnt to cinders. No more running for me.

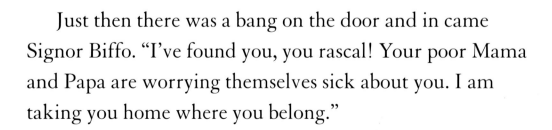

Just then there was a bang on the door and in came Signor Biffo. "I've found you, you rascal! Your poor Mama and Papa are worrying themselves sick about you. I am taking you home where you belong."

When I got home, Mama and Papa were so happy to see me that they forgave me immediately and Papa set to work making me some new feet.

"I'm so hungry," I whispered. "Please can I have some bread?"

"I'm sorry, Pinocchio, but we've only got three pears, one for each of us."

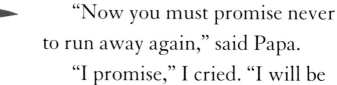

"I want them all, with no skins," I said. When I had finished them, I was still hungry.

"If you were really hungry, you would eat the skins too," said Papa. "Waste not, want not."

So I ate the skins and Papa was right – I wasn't hungry any more.

As soon as my new feet were ready I jumped up and danced around the room.

"Now you must promise never to run away again," said Papa.

"I promise," I cried. "I will be a good boy and I will go to school, but please could you make me some clothes, Mama? It is hard being a puppet with no clothes."

"Of course," she said, and quickly made me a beautiful suit from an old curtain and a hat to match, while Papa made a pair of shoes from an old leather bag.

They were so poor that Papa had to sell his old coat to buy me a book for school. I knew when the winter came Papa would miss his coat. I was very grateful. I ran and hugged him and said, "Thank you, Papa. I love you and I will never let you down. I promise."

Chapter Three

I set off for school, feeling very grand in my new clothes and carrying my new book. On the way I heard a band playing.

I couldn't resist turning round and following the music. In the middle of the square was a huge tent with a sign outside:

The Greatest Puppet Show in the World
Entrance: 4 pennies

But I had no money. How could I get in?

Just then a man beside me said, "My little boy would love a book like yours. If you sell it to me, I will give you four pennies."

I gave the man my book, took the money and slipped into the tent.

And what a show it was!

Punch and Judy, Pierrot and Colombine, a dancing bear and a snapping crocodile – they were all there and they invited me to come up on stage and dance with them! I was a star, but not for long as you will see.

Suddenly a terrible ogre appeared, with yellow teeth and nails like claws.

"Haha!" he boomed. "A wooden puppet, just right to burn in my oven to cook my dinner!"

He was just about to throw me in the oven when I cried out, "Please don't burn me! I am a new kind of puppet, the only one in the world."

"All right," said the ogre, "I'll burn a couple of the other puppets today." And dropping me he picked up Punch and Judy.

"No!" I cried, "These are my friends. If you do this you must throw me on the fire too."

At that the ogre became kinder. "What a brave little puppet you are, how I would love to have a son like you. I shall burn no puppets today. Off you all go, enjoy yourselves!"

And so we did, dancing and singing together as the days were long. But gradually I began to miss Mama and Papa and I knew I must go home.

My friends were sad to see me go and the ogre gave me five gold coins to give Mama and Papa. Everyone hugged me and kissed me and, although I was sad to leave, I knew I was doing the right thing.

Chapter Four

As I set off for home, whistling cheerily to myself, two curious characters came towards me – a blind cat and a lame fox.

"Hello, Pinocchio," they said.

"How do you know my name?" I asked.

"Oh, everyone knows Pinocchio," they said, "because your Mama and Papa ask everyone if they have seen their puppet son, whom they love so much and miss so dreadfully."

Then I felt really bad.

"How are they?" I asked.

"Not so well," Lame Fox replied.

"So well," echoed Blind Cat.

"Your Papa is very cold without his coat," said Lame Fox.

"Without his coat," echoed Blind Cat.

"Papa won't be cold any more when he sees what I've got!" I said.

"What have you got?" asked Lame Fox.

"You got," echoed Blind Cat.

And I showed them my five gold coins.

At that moment a blackbird began to speak in a tree beside the road, "Look out, Pinocchio, these two are tricksters..."

But before he could finish Blind Cat leapt on him and the bird flew away.

"Poor blackbird," I cried, "why did you do that?"

"Don't worry Pinocchio," said Lame Fox, "we have more important things to tell you about."

"Tell you about," echoed Blind Cat.

"Now Pinocchio, about those five gold coins," said Lame Fox.

"Five gold coins," echoed Blind Cat.

"If you come with us to the City of Simple Simons we'll take you to the Field of Wonders. There you can turn your gold into a fortune."

"Into a fortune," echoed Blind Cat.

What a wonderful idea, I thought. *Now Mama and Papa will never have to work again.* And I danced with joy.

"Can we go now?" I cried.

"Of course," said Lame Fox, "just come with us."

"Come with us," echoed Blind Cat.

And off we went together.

Chapter Five

Although we walked for miles, the City of Simple Simons never came any closer. It was getting dark and we were feeling tired when Lame Fox suggested we should stop for the night at the Inn of the Red Lobster.

My new friends managed to eat a good meal, but I was too exhausted to eat very much.

When we went to bed I could hardly sleep. I kept thinking how happy my Mama and Papa were going to be when I came home with a fortune in gold.

I must have gone to sleep eventually. When I woke up the landlord told me my friends had gone ahead and would meet me at the Field of Wonders. They had left a message asking me if I minded paying their bill for the night.

Of course I minded, but I had to pay, didn't I? And anyway, my other gold coins were going to turn into hundreds and thousands at the Field of Wonders, so why worry?

I set off alone to follow my new friends. The road led through a dark forest, full of growlings and snarlings. It was so scary that I whistled to keep up my spirits.

"Don't worry, Pinocchio," said a little voice, and when I looked up I saw a tiny glowing light.

"I am Talking Cricket. Remember?"

"Go away!" I shouted.

"You should go home to your Mama and Papa who cry for you day and night."

"It is none of your business," I shouted, "and anyway, I will go home as soon as I am rich. My four gold coins will become thousands, you'll see."

"You silly puppet. You have to earn your fortune – money doesn't grow on trees, you know."

"Mind your own business! Why should I listen to you?" I cried.

"Because I am your conscience, Pinocchio, and I will always tell you what is right and what is wrong."

"I'll do what I want," I yelled.

"Please yourself, Pinocchio, but watch out for crooks and highwaymen – they are everywhere, be careful."

"Get lost, Talking Cricket," I shouted, and ran off through the dark, scary forest.

I'm not afraid, I told myself, *I am Pinocchio. I don't care.*

Just then, out of the forest came two cloaked figures, both wearing masks, one taller than the other.

These must be the highwaymen Talking Cricket warned me about, I thought.

Quickly I hid my four coins in my mouth, under my tongue.

"Give us your gold," said one.

"Your gold," said the other.

"If you don't hand over your gold, you will never see your Mama and your Papa again," said the small one.

"Your Mama and your Papa again," said the taller one.

"Oh please don't hurt my Mama and my Papa!" I cried.

When they heard the gold coins clinking in my mouth, the highwaymen tried to grab me. I dodged past them, and climbed up into the nearest tree.

I thought I would be safe there. But the two highwaymen lit a fire at the bottom of the tree, and as the flames rose up and the smoke curled around me, I knew I would have to jump.

I leapt down and ran. Imagine my joy when I saw a cottage ahead of me in the woods. I hammered on the door and called out, "Help me, help me. Please open the door!"

A window opened and a beautiful girl looked out. "No one lives here," she whispered.

"I don't care, just let me in! Please help me, I beg you."

But before she could say anything more, the two highwaymen were there, dragging me back into the forest. They tried to open my mouth, but I kept it firmly shut.

"Hang him by his thumbs," said one.

"By his thumbs," said the other.

So they hauled me up into a tree and I hung there, hour after hour, with my mouth firmly shut.

The two highwaymen waited and waited until they got bored.

"We'll be back in the morning," said one.

"In the morning," echoed the other.

I hung there all night thinking how stupid I had been. I longed to see my Mama and Papa once more, to say goodbye and to say how sorry I was.

I closed my eyes.

Chapter Six

The next thing I knew, I was flying through the air, carried in the claws of a huge falcon. We flew over the forest until he dropped me down gently on the mossy ground. Then he rose into the air with a great cry of farewell.

I found myself outside the little cottage where the beautiful girl had spoken to me. This time she took me in and carried me upstairs, singing to me softly.

"I have sent for three of the best doctors to make you well again. One is a cackling crow, one is a hooting owl and the third is a dear friend of mine, Talking Cricket."

I really didn't want to see Talking Cricket again.

Keep quiet, I told myself. *Just keep quiet and pretend to be asleep.*

Neither Cackling Crow nor Hooting Owl could find out what was wrong with me, but Talking Cricket spoke up at once and said, "I know this puppet. He's a runaway who's breaking his Mama's heart and making his Papa's life a misery. He's a headstrong rascal who never takes advice."

Talking Cricket was so right. I began to sob with remorse. When the doctors had gone, Good Fairy bent down and kissed me.

"Sweet dreams," she said, and left.

In my dreams, Good Fairy brought me a bowl of hot soup and sat down beside me and asked me about my adventures.

I told her everything: the ogre, the highwaymen, the golden coins – everything.

"And where are those golden coins now?" she asked.

Oh dear, I thought, *perhaps Good Fairy is not as good as she seems, perhaps she's after my money too?*

"Er – I lost them in the forest," I told her.

At that moment, I felt my noise twitching and stretching itself.

"Anything that's lost can be found," said Good Fairy.

"Er – yes, I remember now. I didn't lose them, I swallowed them with the soup."

My nose was growing longer still, and I hid my face to cover it.

Good Fairy was laughing. "If you lie any more, Pinocchio, your nose will be so long that you won't be able to get out of the door!"

I was so ashamed, I ran for the door to try and get away, but my nose was too long. I couldn't reach the handle.

Good Fairy was right. Talking Cricket had been right. They were both right about everything.

At that moment, a flock of woodpeckers seemed to fill the room. They flew down and began to peck at my nose, and I woke up. I felt my nose. Thank goodness it was still there!

When Good Fairy came in to see me again, I told her of my horrible dream.

"Don't worry, Pinocchio," she said, "I am here now to look after you and take care of you. Your dear Mama and Papa are on their way to be with you too."

"That's wonderful!" I cried. "I'll run down to meet them."

I got up and dressed, stuffing the gold coins in my pockets, and ran out.

I hadn't gone far when I met Lame Fox and Blind Cat.

"Where have you been?" they asked. "Let's go to the Field of Wonders right away and turn your four coins into a fortune."

On the way we went through the City of Simple Simons. It was a sad place. Everyone and everything was miserable and grey. No one smiled or sang.

At last we came to the Field of Wonders.

"Come on, no time to lose," said Lame Fox.

"Time to lose," said Blind Cat.

Quickly they showed me how to plant my four gold coins and water them with water from the stream.

"Just give them an hour or so and a tree full of golden blossom will grow in their place. Now we must be off to help more people to make their dreams come true. Goodbye, goodbye."

"Goodbye, dear friends," I said. "Thank you for all your kindness."

And I sat down to watch and wait.

Chapter Seven

I waited but nothing happened and I fell asleep. I was woken by a Wriggly Worm.

"Who's a Silly Billy?" he whispered.

I was about to squash him when a familiar little voice in my ear said, "Don't do it, Pinocchio." It was the voice of Talking Cricket and for once I took his advice.

"While you were asleep," continued Wriggly Worm, "Lame Fox and Blind Cat dug up your gold coins and ran off."

He was right. I dug where I had planted my coins. They had gone!

In my fury, I was about to stamp on Wriggly Worm but he cried out, "Don't be angry with me, be cross with yourself for being so greedy."

I wanted justice. I went back to the City of Simple Simons, straight to the Court House, and demanded to see the judge.

The judge was a brooding gorilla. When I told him how wicked Lame Fox and Blind Cat had been, he frowned and said, "Prison for ten years it will be. Bread and water only. Not for Lame Fox and Blind Cat. For you, for being so stupid and so lazy."

I lay on the straw in my cell and sobbed. I had let down everyone who had tried to help me, all my good friends and my kind Mama and Papa.

I had to get home, so I tricked the jailer and escaped from the prison. I ran as fast as I could back to Good Fairy's cottage.

On the way I met a terrible monster, a green snaky creature, breathing fire, with eyes like burning coals. He was blocking the way so I turned off and kept running through the trees until I came to a vineyard with luscious grapes hanging down, just within my reach. I was starving. I began to fill my mouth with the delicious fruit.

Suddenly there was a huge CRACK like a pistol shot. I looked down. My leg was caught in a vicious trap. How it hurt! I yelled but no one came.

Then I saw a faint light flickering just in front of me, and I called out, "Please help, I'm caught in a trap! Please help me."

"What happened?" asked the Flickering Firefly.

"I was just eating a few grapes… I was so hungry," I said.

"Stealing more like," she said. "Being hungry is no excuse for taking what is not yours. You must learn by your mistakes." And Flickering Firefly flew away.

When the farmer found me in the morning he was furious. He took me out of the trap and chained me up to a dog kennel.

"I'm not a dog," I complained. "I can't bark."

"Even if you are not a dog, you can guard my chickens from the weasels. When they come you must shout to tell me. Got it?"

When I woke in the middle of the night, I could hear the weasels digging under the fence and I had an idea.

I smiled at the weasels and said, "Why don't I let you all into the
hen run and you can catch all the chickens you need?"

"No barking?" they said.

"Of course not," I replied, and I opened the gate to the hen
yard. As soon as they were all in, I shut the gate again and
shouted, "Mr Farmer, come quickly, I've caught all the weasels
for you!"

The farmer was so pleased with me that he unchained
me and gave me a tasty breakfast of homemade bread and
marmalade before he sent me on my way again.

Chapter Eight

I set off once more to find Good Fairy's cottage. By the end of the day I was no nearer and I lay down under a tree and cried myself to sleep.

I was woken by a Cooing Pigeon. When I had explained who I was, Cooing Pigeon said, "Jump on my back, Pinocchio, and I will take you to find your Mama and Papa and Good Fairy."

I jumped on, lickety split, and Cooing Pigeon carried me over fields and over mountains until we reached the sea.

When I looked down I could see a beach with lots of people and huge waves crashing down on the sand.

When we landed the people came running towards us, shouting, "Look! There's the old man setting out to sea in his tiny boat to find his son Pinocchio. How brave is that?"

I looked out and saw a tiny white boat in the distance. But just then a huge wave towered up and crashed down and the boat disappeared.

Papa! I thought. I rushed into the water and swam towards where the tiny boat had been. Huge waves surged around me and I could see nothing.

Luckily an even bigger wave picked me up and threw me on to a lovely sandy beach. But even so, I felt dreadfully alone and I began to cry.

"Why so downhearted?" came a voice from the sea. It was a Smiling Dolphin who said, "Pinocchio, get up and walk to the village of Busy Bees. Someone will help you there."

I thanked Smiling Dolphin and set off. I walked on, getting hungrier and thirstier. When I arrived at the village of Busy Bees everyone seemed too busy to help me, until I met an old woman carrying two heavy jugs of water.

"Can I have a drink of your water?" I asked.

"If you would help me carry these heavy jugs, I would be happy to give you some water," said the old lady with a smile.

I thought I recognised her voice, but I wasn't sure.

When we got to the old lady's house she took off her bonnet and then I did recognise her. She was Good Fairy! I leapt up and hugged her. How happy I was now.

After a lovely tea of bread and jam and chocolate cake, Good Fairy said, "Pinocchio, it is time for you to go to school like other little boys."

"OK," I said, and off I went.

At school all the children worked really hard, but my new friend Lampwick was just as naughty and lazy as me. He liked getting into fights with the other boys, and I discovered I did too. Mr Beaky the teacher often put us in the corner to punish us, but we didn't mind. We thought it was funny.

One day we got into a fight on the beach, throwing books. It was fun until the police came with a huge dog. I ran off, but the dog came after me, breathing hot breath down my neck and gnashing his huge white teeth.

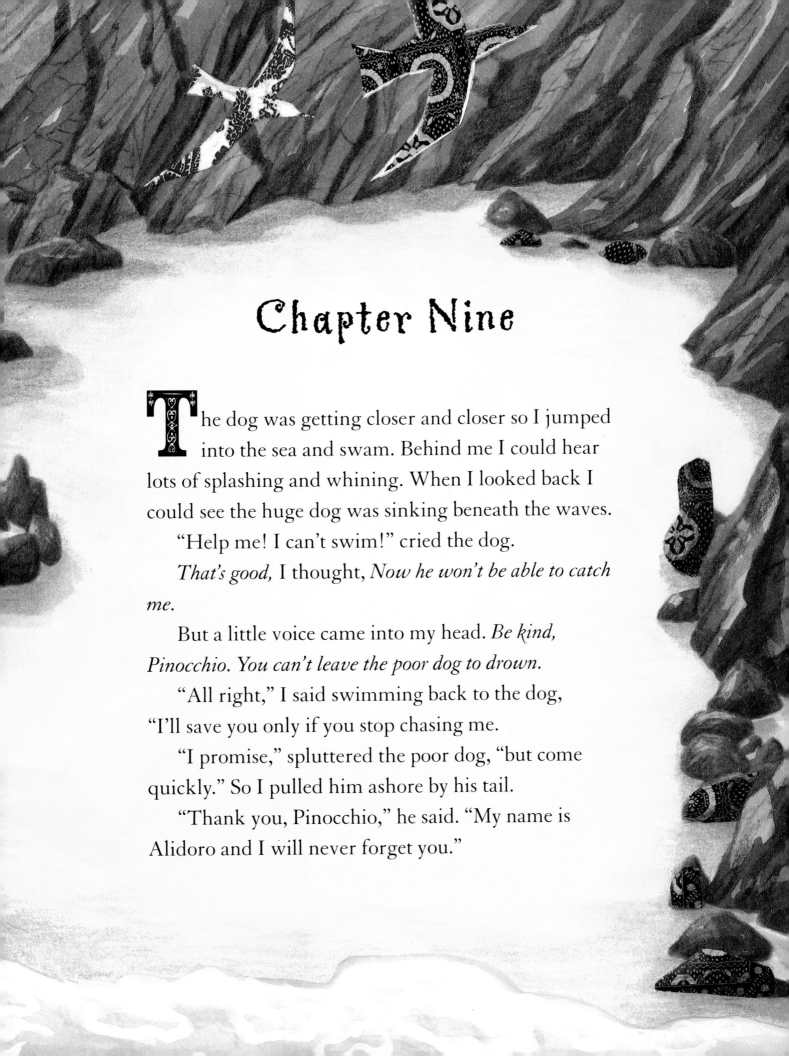

Chapter Nine

The dog was getting closer and closer so I jumped into the sea and swam. Behind me I could hear lots of splashing and whining. When I looked back I could see the huge dog was sinking beneath the waves.

"Help me! I can't swim!" cried the dog.

That's good, I thought, *Now he won't be able to catch me.*

But a little voice came into my head. *Be kind, Pinocchio. You can't leave the poor dog to drown.*

"All right," I said swimming back to the dog, "I'll save you only if you stop chasing me.

"I promise," spluttered the poor dog, "but come quickly." So I pulled him ashore by his tail.

"Thank you, Pinocchio," he said. "My name is Alidoro and I will never forget you."

I swam out to sea again until suddenly I was caught up in a net with lots of fish and hauled out of the water. The next thing I knew I was being thrown into a basket and carried home by an ugly green fisherman.

"What a fine catch. What a meal I will have tonight," said the fisherman.

I could hear the butter sizzling in the pan as he rolled me in flour. I was about to become fish and chips! *This really is the end of me,* I thought.

But just as the green fisherman was dropping me into the pan, a huge dog burst into the cottage. It was Alidoro! The fisherman was so surprised that he dropped me straight into Alidoro's mouth and off we went together.

"Thank you, Alidoro, thank you," I said.

"What are friends for?" he replied. "Didn't you save my life not so long ago? Now off you go, and keep out of trouble."

I went back to apologise to the Good Fairy. I thought that she might be angry with me. But as soon as I told her all that had happened, she hugged me and sat me down to a huge breakfast of pancakes and honey.

At school all my friends welcomed me back. Only Lampwick seemed a bit less pleased.

"What's the matter?" I asked him.

"I'm leaving here. I want you to come with me," he said.

"But where are you going?" I asked.

"To the Land of Toys. It's going to be great, Pinocchio. No more school, holidays every day, just playtime and parties."

"But I promised the Good Fairy I would be good and go to school and never run away again," I said.

"Boring, boring, Pinocchio. Life is for living, for fun, not for working," said Lampwick.

It all sounded so exciting, I couldn't make up my mind.

Just then we heard a bell tinkling and the sound of trotting hooves.

"It's the wagon that will take us to the Land of Toys," said Lampwick. "Make up your mind, Pinocchio. It's now or never – life in the Land of Toys or boring old school every day."

I knew what I was doing was wrong, but at that moment a life of fun and games sounded much better to me than a life of lessons and schoolwork.

And Lampwick was my best friend.

Chapter Ten

When the wagon arrived its wheels made no sound. It was full of happy children. It was pulled by five pairs of grey donkeys and driven by a little fat man with sharp ferrety eyes, who mewed like a cat. I didn't like any of it.

"Hop on, dear children," mewed the little man. "We are off to the Land of Toys. Come with us and be happy for ever."

"I'm not sure," I said. "What would my Good Fairy say? It will break her heart if I run away again."

"Make up your mind," mewed the Little Fat Man. "Can't wait all day. You can ride on a donkey if you like."

Lampwick leapt up on to a donkey, "Come on, Pinocchio, what are you waiting for?"

And up I jumped to the cheers of the children. We all sang songs as the donkeys trotted into the night.

Then I heard a little voice whispering to me. It was my donkey.

"Don't do it, Pinocchio. Jump off and go home before it is too late."

"Shut up, donkey," screeched the Little Fat Man, cracking his whip. "No talking, just pull."

My donkey never spoke again, but I saw big tears running down his face.

"Take no notice," said the Little Fat Man. "By morning we will be in the Land of Toys and you will be happy you came."

And I was. The Land of Toys had everything. We played all day and we stayed up as long as we liked at night. We ate all the foods I loved most – sweets, ice cream, cakes and sausages – and best of all there was no school.

But by and by I began to miss my Mama and Papa and Good Fairy. I wondered how they were.

One morning I woke up feeling a bit strange. I touched my ears. They were long and hairy.

My neighbour Dozy Dormouse took one look at me and said, "Pinocchio, my dear, I'm afraid you've caught the dreaded donkey fever. In a couple of hours you will be a donkey."

"But it's not my fault," I cried. "Lampwick brought me here."

"No, Pinocchio, it *is* your fault. What you do is up to you and no one else." And Dozy Dormouse scuttled away.

I was so ashamed, I put a paper bag over my head to hide my ears and went to see Lampwick. He had a paper bag over his head too.

"Can I see your ears?" I asked.

"If I can see yours," he replied.

We took off the paper bags and saw that we both had donkeys' ears. We burst out laughing, but our laughter sounded like the braying of donkeys.

He-haw, he-haw.

We looked down.

Our feet had turned into hooves and there was fur growing on our legs.

We were donkeys!

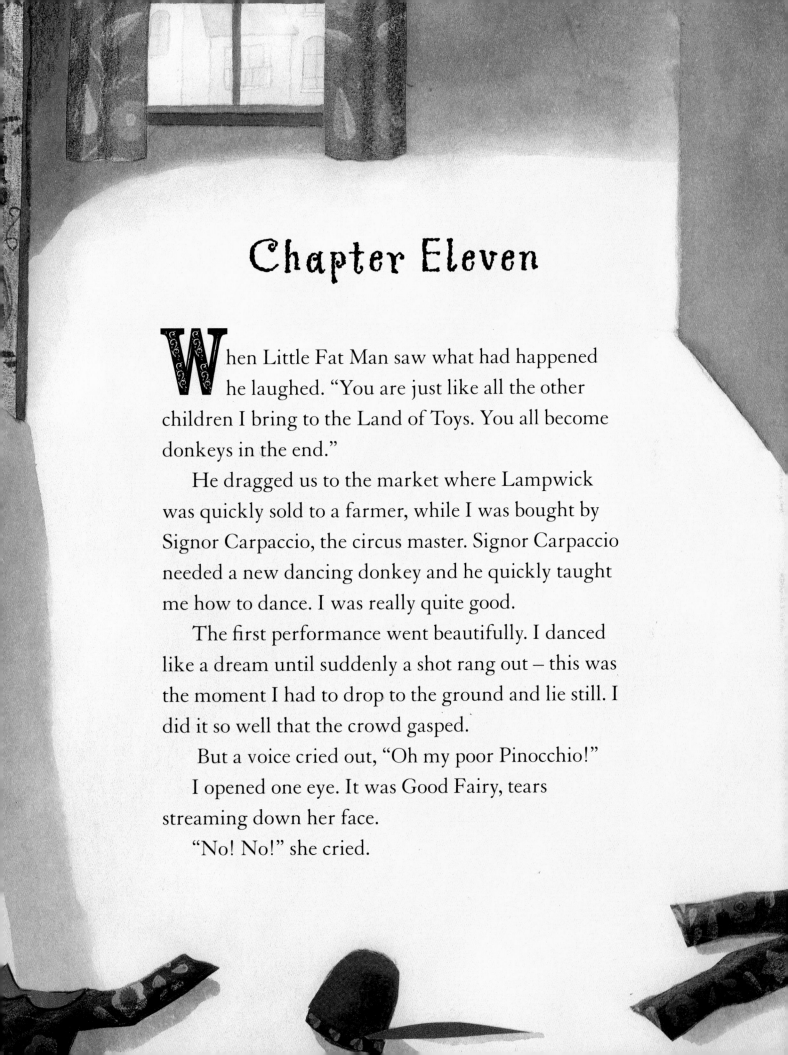

Chapter Eleven

When Little Fat Man saw what had happened he laughed. "You are just like all the other children I bring to the Land of Toys. You all become donkeys in the end."

He dragged us to the market where Lampwick was quickly sold to a farmer, while I was bought by Signor Carpaccio, the circus master. Signor Carpaccio needed a new dancing donkey and he quickly taught me how to dance. I was really quite good.

The first performance went beautifully. I danced like a dream until suddenly a shot rang out – this was the moment I had to drop to the ground and lie still. I did it so well that the crowd gasped.

But a voice cried out, "Oh my poor Pinocchio!"

I opened one eye. It was Good Fairy, tears streaming down her face.

"No! No!" she cried.

I leapt to my feet and galloped towards her. But Signor Carpaccio was after me and whipped me so hard I fell down again. When I looked again my Good Fairy had gone.

Signor Carpaccio had no further use for me now. He sold me off to a drum maker who wanted to use my skin for making drums. He threw me into the sea, tied to the end of a long rope. Down, down I went, right to the bottom of the sea.

This is the end of me, I thought.

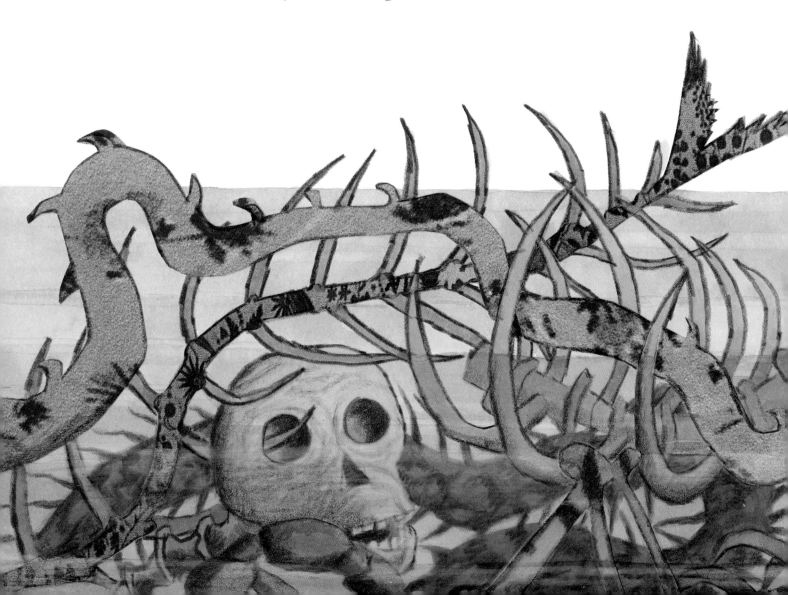

When I woke up I was no longer a donkey. I was Pinocchio once more and now I was inside the stomach of a giant gruesome shark. Sitting beside me was a helpful tuna fish.

"Are we alone?" I asked.

"I think so," whispered Helpful Tuna Fish. "Just you and me and a lot of smelly bones."

"How are we going to get out?" I asked.

"Follow me," whispered Helpful Tuna Fish.

So we set forth together across the vast bony wasteland inside Gruesome Shark's stomach.

Chapter Twelve

Helpful Tuna Fish and I struggled on through the murky waters, following a pinprick of light.

As we drew closer we realised that it was the light of a candle, flickering in the gloom.

Then we saw an old man, sitting with his head in his hands, sobbing, "Oh my poor Pinocchio, where are you, what has become of you?"

My heart leapt. I knew that voice. It was Gepetto, my Papa!

I ran over to him and threw my arms round his neck. "I'm here, Papa, I'm here!'

"Is it really you, Pinocchio? Tell me I am not dreaming!"

At last we were together again. With the help of Helpful Tuna Fish we made our way out of Gruesome Shark's stomach, up his throat and out of his mouth, between his sharp white teeth.

"Follow me," whispered Helpful Tuna Fish.

"Hop on my back, Papa, and hold on tight," I said. "I'll swim us home."

We swam on until we reached dry land, where Helpful Tuna Fish said goodbye and swam away. "Thank you, I will never forget you, I promise," I called after him.

Papa and I started to walk home. On the way we met Lame Fox and Blind Cat. They said they were sorry for all the nasty things they had done to me. Although I didn't really feel like forgiving them, I knew I should, and I did.

We met Talking Cricket, who was still very annoying but I was pleased to see him again.

By the side of the road we came across a farmer beating his donkey with a big stick. I was so angry that I snatched the stick and chased the farmer away. You've guessed it – the poor old donkey was Lampwick! We tended his bruises and gave him some water and he too joined our cavalcade.

When we got home we found Mama waiting at the door to greet us. She threw her arms round me and we hugged – how we hugged. And who was standing beside her but my dear Good Fairy.

I was home at last with everyone I loved in the world.

What I, Pinocchio, have learned from all my adventures is:

Things are never what they seem to be,
Never give up,
And most importantly –
Always be kind.